PERSUASION

JANE AUSTEN

www.realreads.co.uk

Retold by Gill Tavner
Illustrated by Ann Kronheimer

Published by Real Reads Ltd
Stroud, Gloucestershire, UK
www.realreads.co.uk

First published in 2008

ISBN 978-1-906230-07-4

Printed in China by Imago Ltd
Designed by Lucy Guenot
Typeset by Bookcraft Ltd, Stroud, Gloucestershire

CONTENTS

THE CHARACTERS

Anne Elliot

Eight years ago Anne was persuaded to reject the man she loved. Will she now have a second chance to find true love and happiness?

Sir Walter Elliot and Miss Elizabeth Elliot

Anne's father and sister are proud – some think too proud – of their family name. Is their vanity the greatest threat to their future comfort?

Lady Russell

Lady Russell loves Anne like a daughter. Although she is kind, is she wise? Will her persuasive powers once again lead Anne towards heartbreak?

Captain Wentworth

This is the gallant man whose heart Anne broke many years ago. Can he love her again, or will he be charmed by the young and beautiful Louisa Musgrove?

Louisa and Henrietta Musgrove

These two beautiful, lively sisters are in search of husbands. Can either of them mend Captain Wentworth's broken heart?

Mr William Elliot

Why is the handsome heir to Sir Walter Elliot's estate seeking Anne's father's friendship? What are his intentions regarding Anne? Can he be trusted?

Mrs Clay

Why has this young widow befriended Sir Walter and Elizabeth? Are Anne and Lady Russell right to distrust her?

PERSUASION

'Captain Wentworth is nobody!' exclaimed Sir
Walter Elliot, the grand owner of Kellynch Hall.
He placed on the table his huge book in which
all the gentry of England were listed. 'I challenge
you to find his family's name in here.' Anne
didn't try. She knew it wasn't in the book's well-
worn pages. Her father continued, 'Marriage
to a mere naval officer, with neither wealth nor
connections, would be degrading for our family.
Isn't that so, Lady Russell?'

Anne looked up at their neighbour, who had
been as a mother to her since her own mother's
death five years ago.

'It would indeed be a most unfortunate
alliance,' said Lady Russell softly.

Although Anne Elliot was now a beautiful
nineteen-year-old, she felt like a small child as
she stood before these two proud defenders of
rank and honour. Listening to them, she felt her
heart break.

'Anne, you are free to do as you wish,' added Sir Walter, looking into his small hand-mirror and carefully adjusting a stray hair. Pleased with his fine appearance, he continued, 'but if you do degrade the name of Elliot, you shall receive nothing from me. I am astonished that you should even consider marrying such a man.' With a cold look at Anne, he left the room. His haughty eldest daughter, Elizabeth, followed him.

Lady Russell gently took Anne aside. It was true that the proposed marriage threatened the Elliot family name, but she was also concerned about Anne's happiness. Captain Wentworth seemed headstrong and determined – inappropriate characteristics, she felt, for a man of his low standing. Lady Russell needed to prevent the wedding if she could, but she also needed to consider Anne's feelings.

Within a week, Anne had been persuaded that to marry the man she loved and who was deeply in love with her, would be improper, foolish and selfish. Her duty to her family was of paramount importance. Now she had the task of persuading Frederick Wentworth that her refusing his hand was for the best.

That afternoon, Captain Wentworth stared at Anne in dismay and disbelief. 'You have always known that I have only myself to offer. I thought that was enough for you.' Anne could not look at him. 'Anne, I am confident of further success in the navy. We will be rich both in love and in wealth.'

Anne loved his confidence. As she raised her eyes to his handsome, pleading face, she felt that with his intelligence, spirit and brilliance, he would indeed be successful. She struggled to speak. 'I am convinced you will do better if you are free of the need to provide for me.'

'You are convinced? You have been convinced by others! You have yielded to persuasion! I did not think you so weak and indecisive. I thought you stronger.' Anne lowered her eyes again. 'You have been persuaded against your own heart, your own judgement, and your own happiness. I wish you well.'

Angrily, he left the room. Within a short time, he had left the country.

The Elliot name was safe.

Whilst the Elliot name had been saved, unfortunately the Elliot fortune, in the hands of such a vain and extravagant man as Sir Walter, had not.

Eight years passed. For Anne they were years of sadness. With the loss of her true love, she also lost her youthful spirits and her bloom of health, yet her heart remained constant to Captain Wentworth. She regularly scanned the papers for any news of his activities.

For Sir Walter, and for his favourite daughter Elizabeth who resembled him in both looks and manners, the eight years were a time of self-indulgence and lavish spending in maintaining the outward appearance of Elliot grandeur. The sensible influence of Anne's mother, who had guided Sir Walter towards moderation and economy, was long gone. Lady Russell, in spite of her best efforts, had been unable to persuade him to live within his means. She knew his extravagance could not go on.

'Sir Walter, your finances are in disarray,' Lady Russell told her old friend firmly. 'It is vital that you repay your debts.' She took a deep breath. 'I suggest that you reduce your expenses by letting Kellynch Hall, and renting accommodation for yourself and Elizabeth in Bath.' Sir Walter was silent. 'Many of our finest families have done the same. As Bath is such a fashionable city, your decision to be there

will not be questioned.' Sir Walter cast a quick glance towards Anne. 'Anne can stay with her sister Mary at Uppercross Cottage,' concluded Lady Russell.

After days of convincing Sir Walter that other fine men had made the same decision, the matter was settled. Sir Walter Elliot was to quit Kellynch Hall, and a suitable occupant for the estate was quickly secured. Admiral Croft had made his fortune in the navy, and was now ready to enjoy some homely comfort with his wife on dry land.

Sir Walter consoled himself. 'Admiral Croft will not be as admired at Kellynch as I have been. Sailors are so exposed to the climate that their worn faces are not fit to be seen. They should be knocked on the head at the age of forty to prevent such unsightliness.' He observed his reflection in his little mirror with the usual satisfaction. 'Yes, I am to let my home to a grateful inferior.'

Lady Russell and Anne exchanged satisfied smiles. Their relief, however, turned to concern when, after a moment's quiet self-admiration, Sir Walter asked Elizabeth, 'Would you like to bring your friend Mrs Clay to Bath?'

Mrs Clay, the widowed daughter of Sir Walter's lawyer, was a clever young woman who knew the art of flattering the older Sir Walter. Her friendship with Elizabeth had developed quickly and she was now a regular guest at Kellynch. 'She is a most dangerous companion,' Lady Russell had once tried to warn Elizabeth, suspecting that Mrs Clay had designs on Sir Walter's fortune.

Elizabeth had merely laughed. 'Mrs Clay has freckles and a projecting tooth! Were she pretty I might be concerned, but my father is safe from such a face as Mrs Clay's.'

Lady Russell and Anne still distrusted Mrs Clay's motives, especially since Sir Walter was without a direct male heir. In the absence of a son his estate was destined to pass to a nephew, Mr William Elliot. However, should Sir Walter ever remarry and produce a son, that son would inherit everything.

Anne made the arrangements for her father's removal to Bath and her own short journey to Uppercross Cottage. When all was ready, she helped Sir Walter follow Elizabeth into the carriage. Her father wore a slightly puzzled expression. 'Admiral Croft's wife has a brother whose name I am quite sure I have heard before,' he pondered. 'I know the name, but cannot put a face to it at all. Elizabeth, does the name Captain Wentworth mean anything to you?'

Anne's younger sister, Mary, had married Charles Musgrove, the heir to the neighbouring Uppercross Estate. They lived in the grounds of Uppercross Great House, where Charles' parents, Mr and Mrs Musgrove, lived with their daughters Henrietta and Louisa. Anne's removal to Uppercross Cottage took her only a few miles from home. Should Captain Wentworth ever visit his sister, Mrs Croft, at Kellynch, Anne and he were likely to meet.

Admiral Croft and his wife soon became acquainted with the Musgroves of Uppercross, and Anne was pleased to be included in their social circle. Many afternoons saw the same gathering of people at the Great House.

'Oh, Anne, I do not think I am well enough to go to the Great House today,' complained Mary, as she did almost every day.

'I am sorry to hear that,' responded Anne. 'You do not seem to be ill.'

'Oh, I never complain, but today I am more

ill than I have ever been. I am quite unfit to be alone.'

'Then perhaps you should come with me. You would be missed if you stayed at home.' As usual, the flattery worked, and Anne arranged to convey Mary in comfort to Uppercross House.

The company of others offered Anne relief from her sister's limited conversation. The two Miss Musgroves were happy and lively young ladies; their spirits were good and their manners pleasant. Although Anne felt that they lacked some elegance of mind, she enjoyed their energy. For more interesting conversation, Anne sought out Mrs Croft, whom she liked very much.

'I have news for you today, Anne,' said Mrs Croft as she sipped her tea. 'Our circle here is soon to be enlarged. We are expecting a visit from my brother. Were you not acquainted with him some years ago?'

Anne felt her pulse quicken, and hoped that she was too old to blush. She was not, however, too old to feel emotion. Indeed, she was ashamed to feel quite so much after almost eight years. She turned away so that her friend would not notice.

So she would soon meet Captain Wentworth again. It was inevitable.

Now twenty-seven, Anne thought very differently from how she had been taught to think at nineteen. She knew the suffering caused by following caution rather than true love. Furthermore, her searches of the newspapers had informed her that Captain Wentworth had met with the success he had always predicted, and was now a rich man. They could indeed have been wealthy – and happy.

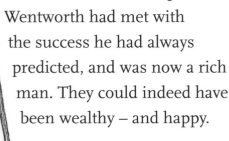

A week passed. Captain Wentworth arrived, and Anne heard that he had paid his first visit to Uppercross House. Louisa and Henrietta Musgrove were delighted. 'He is so much more handsome than any other man we know,' enthused Louisa.

'We are quite in love with him already,' laughed Henrietta. 'He is to dine with us tomorrow, and you are invited too.'

Captain Wentworth was just as anxious about their first meeting as was Anne. He had still not forgiven her for disappointing him. Her weakness and timidity in the face of persuasion had quite disgusted his own decisive, confident temper. Although he had not met anybody who could equal her, he had convinced himself that he could never love Anne Elliot again.

'What do you think of the two lovely Miss Musgroves?' Mrs Croft asked her brother after their first meeting.

'I am ready to marry anybody between

the age of eighteen and thirty if they can offer a little beauty, a few smiles and a few compliments,' smiled Captain Wentworth.

'Your proud eye tells me that this is not quite true. I believe that you value sweetness of temper and sound judgement above all other qualities.'

'Yes,' agreed Captain Wentworth, 'and a strong, decisive mind.'

The following evening, the newly enlarged party gathered at Uppercross House. Anne trembled as Captain Wentworth entered the room. If his looks had changed at all over the past eight years, it was only to gain a greater appearance of robust health.

Captain Wentworth greeted Anne with cold politeness and ceremonious grace. Their eyes half met, he bowed and she curtseyed. They did not speak beyond their initial greeting.

'At least the worst is now over,' Anne consoled herself as she prepared for bed that

evening. As she lay, unable to get to sleep, her reflections became more sombre. They had once meant so much to each other, and now they were nothing. Their hearts had been so open, their faces so dear to each other, and now they were strangers. The hardest thing to bear was his cold politeness.

It was a bright November morning. The party had engaged to meet again for an early walk. Anne fell into step with Mary's husband Charles. Ahead, Captain Wentworth walked arm in arm with both Louisa and Henrietta.

'He would be an excellent match for either of my sisters,' observed Charles Musgrove. Anne had to agree. Captain Wentworth would be an excellent match for anybody. Although the thought of him marrying caused Anne some painful agitation, she did not, upon reflection, believe that he would fall seriously in love with either girl. She was surprised that he was showing them so much attention.

'Of course, we all believe that Henrietta will soon marry our cousin,' continued Charles, unaware of Anne's thoughts. 'She wishes to call upon him during our walk.'

The cousin was duly called upon, invited to join them, and soon took Captain Wentworth's place at Henrietta's side. The couple dropped back a little from the main party, leaving Louisa free to enjoy Captain Wentworth's attentions all to herself.

'I don't know why Henrietta hesitates to accept my cousin's proposal,' Louisa confided in Captain Wentworth. 'If I loved a man I should wish always to be with him. If I had decided to marry a man, nothing would stand in my way.'

Captain Wentworth looked at her admiringly. 'I honour your firm and decisive character,' he said thoughtfully. 'A yielding, indecisive character can never be depended upon.' He bent down to pick a hazelnut from the ground. Charles Musgrove had left Anne's side in pursuit of one of his dogs. She now walked alone. Without meaning to, she caught up with Captain Wentworth and Louisa, and so could not help overhearing the rest of their conversation.

Holding the hazelnut in the palm of his hand, Captain Wentworth began, 'This beautiful glossy nut, blessed with its natural strength, has survived the storms of autumn. It shows no blemish or weakness, and must be as happy as any nut can be.' Louisa laughed, delighted. Looking at her smiling face, Captain Wentworth continued, 'If, like this little nut, you would keep your beauty and happiness for the rest of your life, you must also preserve your strong mind.'

Words of such warm admiration for Louisa caused Anne acute pain. She also felt that she now understood his opinion of her own seemingly weak character. She began to feel weary.

'Miss Elliot, you appear tired.' Anne was startled. Captain Wentworth had left Louisa and appeared at her side. He offered his arm, and supported her in silence for the rest of the walk home. Anne was touched by his kindness. Although he might not have forgiven her, he had noticed her and could not be entirely unfeeling.

Louisa was in very high spirits when she visited Anne the following day. 'Oh, Anne, Henrietta is to marry our cousin. She accepted him on our walk yesterday.'

Anne expressed her pleasure at this news.

Louisa changed the subject. 'Don't you think Captain Wentworth is gallant?'

Anne agreed.

'Mind you, he was not very gallant about you yesterday,' she laughed. 'He says that you have changed so much since he last met you that he can hardly recognise you.'

Knowing nothing of the past, Louisa could not have known the pain that she was causing.

When she left, Anne looked in the mirror. She looked tired, quite worn down by eight years of sadness and regret.

Captain Wentworth had a close friend, Captain Benwick, who lived in the delightful coastal town of Lyme Regis. When Louisa learned this, she proposed that everybody should make a two-day trip to Lyme. The adventure would be exciting. Encouraged by Captain Wentworth's praise of her strong mind, Louisa quickly overcame all obstacles to the visit, and within days Anne found herself in Lyme Regis.

A visit to the coast was a rare treat for Anne. The novelty of the occasion, her love of fresh air, and exposure to the sea wind all helped to restore bloom and freshness to her pretty features. As the party walked up the steps from the seafront and back towards their lodgings on the first afternoon of their visit, they made way for a gentleman who was walking in the opposite direction. As he passed, Anne caught his eye. He paused and looked at her with earnest admiration. Captain Wentworth noticed the gentleman's attention, and immediately looked at Anne himself. For the first time in eight years he saw again the Anne Elliot he had loved.

The next morning was bright and breezy, so once more they all walked down to the sea. Louisa, with the enthusiasm of a small child, jumped from the steps to be caught in Captain Wentworth's arms.

'Louisa, I am afraid that you will hurt yourself, you must not jump again!' cautioned Captain Wentworth.

'Oh, but I will,' cried out Louisa. 'Here I come!' Captain Wentworth caught her again.

'One more time!' she pleaded. Reluctantly, he agreed.

This time, however, she jumped before Captain Wentworth was ready. Everybody watched in horror as Louisa fell to the ground, where she lay motionless.

'She is dead!' cried Henrietta, and fainted with shock.

Captain Wentworth knelt next to Louisa in despair. 'Oh god, is there no one to help?'

Quickly recovering from her initial shock, Anne sent Captain Benwick, who knew the town well, in pursuit of a doctor. She told Mary and Charles to take Henrietta home. She herself waited with Captain Wentworth.

'Oh, if only I had not been persuaded by her!' he groaned. 'This is my fault. Dear, sweet Louisa!'

The doctor arrived quickly; his diagnosis was reassuring. He had seen worse cases of concussion, and was confident that Louisa would recover. She must, however, not be removed from Lyme, and must receive constant care and attention.

Decisions were made quickly. Captain Wentworth was to stay with Captain Benwick. Some other friends in Lyme, Captain and Mrs

Harville, would care for Louisa. Louisa's parents would have to be told as soon as possible. Who should be given this heavy responsibility?

'I can think of no one so capable, so gentle, as Anne,' recommended Captain Wentworth, speaking with a degree of warmth which seemed almost to restore the past.

As she travelled back to Uppercross with Henrietta, Anne found comfort in the knowledge that Captain Wentworth still felt some respect – and perhaps even a degree of fondness – for her. At the same time, she dreaded the news that might soon follow her on the same journey. Would a wedding be planned upon Louisa's recovery? Would Captain Wentworth and Louisa return glowing with all the bright, prosperous love that was so missing from her own life?

Anne's stay at Uppercross was very short. She arranged for Louisa's parents to travel to Lyme, and spent some time with Lady Russell.

'A match between Louisa and Captain Wentworth would be a fine thing,' mused Lady Russell as they sat down to catch up on news. She searched Anne's face for signs of emotion, but Anne had become an expert at composing herself. Lady Russell felt relieved. 'Do you know who has visited your father in Bath recently?' she asked Anne, hardly able to conceal her pleasure.

'No, who?' Anne asked, showing more interest than she felt. Her mind was in Lyme, not in Bath.

'Mr William Elliot.'

'Father's heir? My cousin?'

'The very same.'

'But relations between him and my father have been so poor. I thought they were never to meet again.'

'It seems that Mr Elliot wishes to restore relations. They have dined together several times. I would not be surprised if he were seeking a match with Elizabeth. It would indeed be a fine thing for one of Sir Walter Elliot's daughters to continue as mistress of Kellynch Hall.'

Anne reflected that this was a very probable reason for Mr Elliot's new friendliness towards her father.

'Anne, I am quite tired of the countryside,' sighed Lady Russell. 'I have decided to spend

some time in Bath. Would you like to join me?
Your father says there is room for you in his
lodgings. I shall be staying just around the
corner.'

'Is Mrs Clay still there?' asked Anne,
remembering her earlier concern.

'I'm afraid she is.'

Upon Anne's arrival in Bath, Sir Walter and
Elizabeth were both keen to introduce her to
their new acquaintances.

'It is rather surprising that we have managed
to make some handsome acquaintances,'
explained Sir Walter, 'as most of the women here
are frightful and the men are all scarecrows.
I counted eighty women pass me yesterday
without any one of them being
pretty. Even Mrs Clay is prettier
than most. Bath has given her new
beauty. Her freckles have faded.'

Anne saw Mrs Clay smile. She decided to change the subject and asked her father, 'How do you find Mr Elliot?'

'He is a fine gentleman. You shall meet him tonight.'

As soon as she set eyes on Mr Elliot that evening, Anne gasped in disbelief. It was the same man. The man who had so admired her when they passed briefly on the sea front at Lyme. When Sir Walter introduced her to him, Anne was amused to see Mr Elliot's equal

astonishment as he too recognised her. His eyes showed his pleasure.

The next day, Anne visited Lady Russell. Lady Russell smiled as Anne told her about the chance encounter in Lyme. Her smile broadened as Anne described the previous evening. 'I was surprised that my first social event in Bath passed so pleasantly,' said Anne. 'Mr Elliot's manners were polished and relaxed. He was very agreeable.'

'What do you now think are his intentions?'

'I can only imagine that he wishes to marry Elizabeth.'

Lady Russell smiled again.

Several days passed, during which Anne grew accustomed to the social whirl of Bath. When she discovered that a former schoolfriend, Mrs Smith, was also in Bath, Anne did not hesitate to call upon her to renew their friendship.

Although Mrs Smith had fallen upon hard times, she was clever and lively, and was able to converse about a wide range of subjects. Anne enjoyed her company more than that of any of her father's more impressively-titled friends.

Mr Elliot was a regular visitor to Sir Walter's apartments. Lady Russell watched him with interest. 'I agree with you,' she told Anne. 'His understanding seems good and his heart is warm. I like him.' However, she could not agree with Anne that he intended to marry Elizabeth. 'I no longer think that Elizabeth will be the next Lady Elliot of Kellynch,' she told Anne. 'Mr Elliot told me that he considers you to be a model of female excellence. How wonderful it would be to see you occupy your mother's place as mistress of Kellynch Hall.'

Anne was quiet for a moment. Although Lady Russell's reference to her mother had touched her heart, Mr Elliot had not. Her heart was still Captain Wentworth's. 'Mr Elliot and I would not suit,' she told Lady Russell.

She could not tell her any more. She could not say that she loved another, nor could she explain that Mr Elliot's manners were too polished, too generally acceptable. Could a man who never said anything careless, whose tongue never slipped, be truly sincere? Could he be trusted?

'I will endeavour to persuade you to think as I do,' said Lady Russell. 'In Mr Elliot I see only perfection.'

The following day brought with it two surprises of such significance to Anne that her resulting agitation, pleasure, delight and misery were almost impossible to bear.

The first surprise was news of Louisa's return to Uppercross. Out of any danger from her fall, Louisa was accompanied not by Captain Wentworth, as Anne had so dreaded, but by his old friend Captain Benwick. Captain Benwick had attended the sick Louisa with great devotion, and had won her love as his reward. With Louisa's father's consent, the two could now look forward to a happy marriage.

Anne could barely believe it when told the news. Her cheeks flushed and she rushed away to compose herself. She felt joy, senseless joy. Captain Wentworth was free. She wondered how he felt about the news of Louisa's engagement. She wondered when she might see him again.

The second surprise came that afternoon as Anne, exiting a shop ahead of Elizabeth and Mr Elliot, walked straight into Captain Wentworth as he passed by with another gentleman. Although astonished to find him in Bath, Anne was able to compose herself more quickly than he. Confused and embarrassed, Captain Wentworth greeted her briefly, then walked on. A moment later she saw him stop, leave his friend, and come towards her. He was about to speak when Mr Elliot appeared at Anne's side.

Captain Wentworth's face showed that he recognised Mr Elliot from Lyme. He bowed in confusion before hurrying to rejoin his friend. 'Who is that gentleman?' he asked.

'Of course, you cannot know. That is Mr Elliot. He is the talk of the town. They say he is very fond of his cousin Anne. We can easily guess what will happen there!'

Captain Wentworth and his friend continued their walk in silence.

Anne longed to talk to Captain Wentworth, but did not know when she would next see him. Her opportunity came when she attended a concert several evenings later. Remembering Captain Wentworth's love of music, she was not surprised to see him there. He walked over to greet her.

'We have not spoken since that dreadful event in Lyme,' he began. Anne felt that he looked a little uncomfortable as he continued. 'I am sure that you have heard the news about Benwick and Louisa Musgrove.' Anne nodded. 'I wish them great happiness. I believe they are very much in love.'

Anne looked questioningly into his eyes. Seeing no sign of recent disappointment, she had the confidence to express her surprise at the news.

'They are fortunate in that they will face no opposition,' sighed Captain Wentworth. 'They are free to love, and will not have to endure years of devotion to a person they cannot have. A man never recovers from such devotion.'

Anne was silent and confused, her breathing rapid. Captain Wentworth looked as though he would continue, but they were interrupted by the appearance of Mr Elliot.

'Oh, Miss Elliot, there you are. We must take our seats immediately.' He ushered Anne towards her seat as the music began. She turned to smile apologetically at Captain Wentworth, but he had already turned away. Although frustrated by the interruption, Anne's eyes shone with happiness. She finally knew something of Captain Wentworth's feelings.

Searching the theatre for Captain Wentworth's face, Anne hardly noticed when the first piece of music ended and Mr Elliot took her hand. 'My dear cousin,' he began.

Anne directed her eyes reluctantly towards him.
This was most unwelcome attention. 'The name
of Anne Elliot has long interested me,' he said
softly. 'I wish that it might stay the same upon
her marriage.'

Anne was distressed. Fortunately, the
music began again, preventing Mr Elliot from
completing his speech. At the next interval, Anne
politely excused herself to stretch her legs a little.
After a few minutes of searching, she came across
Captain Wentworth again. He seemed inexplicably
grave. Something must be the matter.

'I have decided to retire for the evening,' he frowned. It was clear that their earlier conversation was not to be continued.

'Is something wrong?' asked Anne.

Captain Wentworth's features softened a little. He seemed about to speak when Mr Elliot once again appeared and placed a possessive hand upon Anne's arm. 'Miss Elliot, you are forever dashing away. The music is about to resume.'

'Won't you join us for the next piece?' Anne asked Captain Wentworth.

'No, there is nothing worth my staying for,' he said hurriedly. 'Goodnight.'

Anne felt sad, but a gentle smile slowly spread across her face. Captain Wentworth was jealous!

Mrs Smith tried very hard to appear pleased for Anne when she visited the following morning. 'Your happy face tells me that the rumour is true. You are to marry your cousin Mr Elliot!'

'My dear Mrs Smith, it is not true at all. It is not Mr Elliot who has made me smile.' Anne detected both relief and curiosity in her friend's features.

'Are you sure that you will not marry Mr Elliot?'

'Perfectly sure. Why do you appear relieved? What do you know of my cousin?'

'Oh, Anne, I have known him for many years.'

Anne sat down and listened with great interest and increasing horror to Mrs Smith's story. Mr Elliot had been a close friend of her late husband, but had heartlessly led him into debt. He had used people badly and lived selfishly. As the executor of Mr Smith's will, he should have released enough money for his friend's widow to live in comfort for the rest of her life but, by failing to do this, he had trapped her in poverty and hardship.

'But why do you think he has repaired relations with my father? He is to inherit Kellynch whether father approves or not.'

'He heard about Elizabeth's friend, Mrs Clay. She is a great danger to his interests. If your father marries her, Mr Elliot could lose Kellynch.

Perhaps he hopes to persuade Sir Walter against a future marriage. His argument that Kellynch should be kept in the family would undoubtedly be made stronger by his own marriage to you.'

Anne was silent. Had she not heard this, was it possible that over time Lady Russell might have persuaded her to accept Mr Elliot's proposal? The thought made her tremble.

Following her conversation with Mrs Smith, Anne found it very difficult to be civil to Mr Elliot. She grew desperate to talk to Captain Wentworth. Whenever she saw him, he looked sad. Whenever she smiled at him, he did not return the smile. Whenever she tried to talk to him, they were interrupted.

Admiral and Mrs Croft, having recently arrived for a stay in Bath, decided to host a dinner. Following the meal, Admiral Croft asked Captain Wentworth to write a quick letter on his behalf.

Anne found herself in conversation with the Admiral, right next to the desk at which Captain Wentworth was writing.

'Kellynch Hall is proving a wonderful home for us,' smiled Admiral Croft. 'You must miss it very much.'

'Since my mother died,' replied Anne, 'it has meant less to me than it might.'

'I understand. A home is only as precious as those within it. For me, nowhere would be home without Mrs Croft. We cannot bear to be apart. Whenever I leave port, she travels with me. The discomforts of a ship are nothing as long as we are together.'

'That is a great credit to you both,' smiled Anne. 'I suspect that many wives' hearts are broken when their husbands sail away.'

'It is not only the wives. We men suffer terribly when separated from our loved ones. Our feelings prey upon us. I believe that you forget us more quickly than we forget you.'

Anne noticed that Captain Wentworth had stopped writing. He appeared to be listening. 'I cannot agree with your last point,' she told

Admiral Croft. 'I believe that women love longer than men, even when all hope is gone.'

A clattering sound attracted Anne's attention. Captain Wentworth had dropped his pen. As he bent to pick it up, he smiled briefly at Anne before resuming his task at the desk. After a few minutes, he appeared at Anne's side.

'Admiral Croft, I have completed your letter. I must now take my leave. I have business to attend to before I sleep.' He bowed politely to Anne, and left the room. Anne did not know how he had managed it, but somehow Captain Wentworth had slipped a folded piece of paper into her hand.

The rest of the evening passed slowly. Anne held in her hand a letter that might decide whether she was to be happy or miserable for the rest of her life. When would she be able to read it?

Dear Anne,

You pierce my soul. You have just told Admiral Croft that a woman never stops loving. This has given me hope. For eight and a half years I have loved only you. I have been resentful, but never inconstant. Now, I once again offer you my heart, which is even more your own than when you broke it all those years ago. A smile or a frown from you will tell me whether I am to be happy.

Frederick Wentworth

Although Anne's overpowering happiness meant that she was quite unable to sleep that night, her eyes were still shining when Captain Wentworth called the next morning. He knew her answer immediately.

They walked together for several hours, sharing the same promises as eight years ago, but this time with even greater tenderness and with greater confidence in their love.

'I believe that I was right to be persuaded by Lady Russell,' said Anne. 'Her advice was wrong, but I was not wrong to be dutiful.'

'I feared that she might persuade you to marry Mr Elliot,' confessed Captain Wentworth. 'I was very jealous.'

'And I was afraid that you would love Louisa,' replied Anne.

'I did try, but how could I love her when your presence constantly reminded me of your superiority?'

This time, Captain Wentworth's wealth reduced Sir Walter's opposition to the match. Poor Lady Russell had to struggle to overcome her prejudice, and to accept that her mistake had caused eight years of unnecessary suffering.

Mr Elliot, his position weakened, needed to find a new way of removing the danger posed to his inheritance by Mrs Clay. How could he prevent her marrying Sir Walter? He charmed her. He persuaded her. They left Bath together, she with hopes of becoming the future Lady Elliot rather than the present one, he with only dishonourable intentions, the chief of which

was to ruin her chances of winning Sir Walter's hand.

Captain Wentworth helped Mrs Smith to recover the money to which Mr Elliot had proved such an obstacle. Over time, he warmed towards Lady Russell and forgave her harmful persuasion.

Who could fail to forgive a person who had had only Anne's happiness in mind, and who now shared so fully in the great happiness of two constant hearts finally united?

TAKING THINGS FURTHER

The real read

This *Real Read* version of *Persuasion* is a retelling of Jane Austen's magnificent work. If you would like to read the full novel in all its original splendour, many complete editions are available, from bargain paperbacks to beautifully-bound hardbacks. You may well find a copy in your local charity shop.

Filling in the spaces

The loss of so many of Jane Austen's original words is a sad but necessary part of the shortening process. We have had to make some difficult decisions, omitting subplots and details, some important, some less so, but all interesting. We have also, at times, taken the liberty of combining two events into one, or of giving a character words or actions that originally belong to another. The points below will fill in some of the gaps, but nothing can beat the original.

- Sir Walter Elliot's large book, *The Baronetcy*, gives the history of England's wealthiest families. Sir Walter often looks at the Elliot family's page.

- Wealth and titles could not normally be inherited by daughters. Instead, an estate would pass to the nearest male relative. In the case of Kellynch, this is Mr William Elliot.

- In the past, Sir Walter had hoped that William Elliot would marry Elizabeth. However, William snubbed Elizabeth and never contacted the family again. This was a great insult.

- Sir Walter's youngest daughter, Mary, married Charles Musgrove, who would eventually inherit the Uppercross estate. Charles had wanted to marry Anne, but she turned down his proposal because she still loved Captain Wentworth. Captain Wentworth is encouraged when Louisa tells him that Anne has rejected Charles's proposal.

- Admiral and Mrs Croft have a very happy and mutually respectful marriage, which Jane Austen invites us to admire.

- Sir Walter does not approve of the wealth of naval officers returning from war. He feels that it threatens social stability.

- During his time in the navy, Captain Wentworth had the Musgroves' son Dick on his ship. Dick is now dead, but his parents are very grateful to Captain Wentworth for his help.

- When Captain Wentworth notices Anne's tiredness on the walk, he arranges for her to be taken home by Admiral and Mrs Croft.

- Captain Benwick's fiancée died, and he is still heartbroken when we first meet him.

- Captain Wentworth does not stay long in Lyme when Louisa is ill. He is aware that he has allowed Louisa to develop expectations of their future marriage, but when he realises that he still loves Anne he hopes that his absence will help to ease the situation.

- Mrs Smith went to school with Anne. She and her husband have lived extravagantly, and she is now a crippled, poor widow.

- Sir Walter and Elizabeth continue to snub Captain Wentworth in Bath, causing Anne pain.

- The conversation Captain Wentworth overhears when writing his letter is really between Anne and Captain Harville. They begin by discussing Benwick's love for Louisa so soon after the death of his fiancée. This allows Anne to make the comment that women's affections survive longer than those of men.

Back in time

Finished in 1816, *Persuasion* was Jane Austen's last completed novel. She died the following year.

When reading any of Jane Austen's novels, it is important to understand the relationship between marriage and wealth. As Anne will not inherit any of her father's wealth, her best chance of an independent and comfortable future is to marry well. Though this may be one of Lady Russell's concerns in persuading Anne to reject Captain Wentworth's offer of marriage, it is certainly not Sir Walter's prime concern.

Sir Walter objects to naval officers because they are not from families of consequence. The navy at the time offered men from modest backgrounds the opportunity to achieve a good reputation and make their fortune. Sir Walter considers this a threat. Jane Austen, however, had great respect for the men who served in the navy.

More than any of her other novels, *Persuasion* is set at a very specific time in history. A short period of peace during the Napoleonic Wars with France allowed naval officers to return home. Readers at the time would have understood that *Persuasion's* happy ending is overshadowed by the fact that Captain Wentworth, Admiral Croft and Captain Benwick would soon have had to return to war.

There are three main locations in *Persuasion* – Kellynch, Bath and Lyme Regis. Sir Walter's move to Bath was typical of the time. Bath was then a highly fashionable place to visit, a place for amusement, romance and adventure for the upper classes.

Finding out more

We recommend the following books and websites to gain a greater understanding of Jane Austen's England:

Books

- Gill Hornby, *Who was Jane Austen? The Girl with the Magic Pen*, Short Books, 2005.

- Jon Spence, *Becoming Jane Austen*, Hambledon Continuum, 2007.

- Josephine Ross, *Jane Austen's Guide to Good Manners: Compliments, Charades and Horrible Blunders*, Bloomsbury, 2006.

- Dominique Enwright, *The Wicked Wit of Jane Austen*, Michael O'Mara, 2007.

- Lauren Henderson, *Jane Austen's Guide to Romance: The Regency Rules*, Headline, 2007.

- Deirdre Le Faye, *Jane Austen: The World of Her Novels*, Frances Lincoln, 2003.

- Tom Tierney, *Fashions of the Regency Period Paper Dolls*, Dover, 2000.

- Caroline Sanderson, *A Rambling Fancy: In the Footsteps of Jane Austen*, Cadogan, 2006.

Websites

- www.janeausten.co.uk
Home of the Jane Austen Centre in Bath, England.

- www.jane-austens-house-museum.org.uk
Jane Austen's home in Hampshire is now a wonderful museum. Here she wrote *Persuasion*, *Mansfield Park* and *Emma*.

- www.janeaustensoci.freeuk.com
Home of the Jane Austen Society. Includes summaries of, and brief commentaries on, her novels.

- www.pemberley.com
A very enthusiastic site for Jane Austen enthusiasts.

- www.literaryhistory.com/19thC/AUSTEN
A selective and helpful guide to links to other Jane Austen sites.

Films

- *Persuasion* (1995), directed by Roger Michell, BBC/2 Entertain Video

- *Persuasion* (2007), directed by Adrian Shergold, BBC/2 Entertain Video.

Food for thought

Here are some things to think about if you are reading *Persuasion* alone, or ideas for discussion if you are reading it with friends.

In retelling *Persuasion* we have tried to recreate, as accurately as possible, Jane Austen's original plot and characters. We have also tried to imitate aspects of her style. Remember, however, that this is not the original work; thinking about the points below, therefore, can help you begin to understand Jane Austen's craft. To move forward from here, turn to the full-length version of *Persuasion* and lose yourself in her wonderful portrayals of human nature

Starting points

- Which character interests you the most? Why?

- What do you think about Jane Austen's choice of Anne Elliot as a heroine? Does your opinion of Anne change as you read the novel?

- What clues can you find about Sir Walter Elliot's personality? How do you feel about him?

- Why do you think Lady Russell was able to persuade Anne not to marry Captain Wentworth? Was Anne right or wrong to be persuaded?

- Did you ever think that Captain Wentworth would marry Louisa?

- What do you think of Mrs Clay and Mr Elliot?

- Who do you think is more gentlemanly – Captain Wentworth, Sir Walter, or Mr Elliot?

Themes

What do you think Jane Austen is saying about the following themes in *Persuasion*?

- family honour

- persuasion

- people who inherit money and people who earn money

- what makes 'an English gentleman'
- love and marriage

Style

Can you find paragraphs containing examples of the following?

- a person exposing their true character through something they say
- humour
- gentle irony, where the writer makes the reader think one thing whilst saying something different – this is often a way of gently mocking one of the characters
- the author's opinion made clear through the writing

Look closely at how these paragraphs are written. What do you notice? Can you write a paragraph in the same style?